The Coelura

The
Coelura

Anne McCaffrey

TOR

THE COELURA

Copyright © 1983, 1987 by Anne McCaffrey
Illustrations © 1987 by Ned Dameron

By arrangement with Underwood/Miller

First Tor Printing: December 1987

A TOR Book

Published by Tom Doherty Associates, Inc.
49 West 24 Street
New York, N.Y. 10010

ISBN: 0-312-93042-9

Library of Congress Catalog Card Number: 87-50872

Printed in the United States of America

0 9 8 7 6 5 4 3 2 1

*This book is dedicated
with respect and affection
to my good neighbor
Maureen Beirne*

"It is your exalted sire," Trin told Lady Caissa in an apprehensive voice. The elderly dresser bobbed up and down with agitation. "He is dressed for hunting but wishes a word with you."

"Then it can't be too serious," Caissa replied, smiling to reassure the nervous woman. She threw an opaque wrap about her and strode through the veiled portal to her reception room.

Though her bare feet made little sound

in the deep pile of the floor covering, the athletic figure of her sire whirled from his inspection of a tri-dimensional labyrinth table game into a hunter's stance.

Caissa smiled at his reflex and made the obeisance proper for the body-heir of Baythan, Minister Plenipotential of the Federated Sentient Planets to Demeathorn, fourth planet of the Star, Cepheus Two.

As Baythan straightened from his alert half-crouch, he fiddled unnecessarily with an armband of stun-darts, a sign to Caissa that her sire had more on his mind than hunting.

"You have, of course, heard that Cavernus Moneor has died. . . ." Baythan turned back to his scrutiny of the labyrinth.

"And his body-heir is already thinking of an heir-contract?" asked Caissa, accurately divining the reason for her sire's fidgets.

"As usual, daughter of my flesh, you are blunt to the point of discourtesy," Baythan replied, regarding her with his notable air of censure.

"No discourtesy, noble sire, was intended."

"None taken, I suppose. I ran a check on the new Cavernus's genetic patterns and find no significant recessives that might combine unfavorably with yours."

Caissa gave her sire a long hard look.

"Cavernus Gustin may be genetically sound, my sire, but he is inept in the hunt to the point of cowardice and almost incoherent save for the formal phrases which have been dinned into what he uses for a brain. Even then, he's apt to come out with inappropriate replies. His haste is precipitous, his choice distasteful to me."

"I have certain reasons," and Baythan drew himself to his full height, a movement that displayed his superb physique and emphasized a naturally proud mien, "which I cannot at this juncture reveal even to you, why an alliance with Cavernus Gustin would, in the not too distant future, be profoundly advantageous. I think I am correct in my belief that you would prefer to remain on Demeathorn rather than take up the star-hopping life your womb-mother prefers?"

"Have you been reassigned, sire?" asked

Caissa, startled by Baythan's vagueness rather than his recommendation.

"I have not been recalled — yet," replied Baythan. Despite his bland expression, Caissa caught a hint of bitterness in his voice that she had rarely heard. "There is, and I mention this in the strictest of secrecy," and Baythan's urbane smile compounded Caissa's confusion, "a possibility that I may satisfactorily complete the mission which first brought me to Demea-thorn."

"As your body-heir, may details of that mission now be imparted to me?" asked Caissa as indifferently as possible, though every ounce of her slender body tensed with expectation.

"When I have concluded my arrangements, yes. Both you and your womb-mother will know. Indeed so shall the galaxy!" His voice had a ring of triumph long delayed. Then his tone changed to the lightly persuasive one that she had heard him use to much advantage and she became wary. "An heir-contract need last only long enough to produce a healthy child, daugh-

ter. Believe me, when I say," and his tone became more urgent, "that a small sacrifice today might reap unexpected rewards . . . tomorrow. However," and Baythan's careless gesture of resignation told Caissa more graphically than any ardent argument how important this proposal was to him, "it will be your decision, my heir."

"I shall give the matter my careful consideration, my sire," she said, bowing her head and making the submission obeisance with her right hand.

"You'd win this game by playing black to white's 4S," he said, making the move on the labyrinth board and smiling at her with gentle condescension.

In a glance, she saw that Baythan was correct but then, he was as accomplished a gamesmaster as he was a hunter.

"You have been a joy to me since your conception, daughter Caissa," Baythan said, stepping forward and gripping her shoulders. He gave her an unexpected paternal kiss on her forehead.

"My sire," she said in surprise for demonstrations of affection were rare. This Ca-

vernus contract must be exceedingly important. She bowed again, in the full display of
filial acknowledgment, crossing her arms
over her breasts, her fingertips touching the
body-heir tattoo that entwined the base of
her throat.

She remained in that position until she
heard her father departing. Then she raised
her head to see him, with a triumphant
swagger to his shoulders, stride through the
thick privacy veil of her reception room.

She exhaled on a deep puzzled note and
slowly walked to the air-cushioned lounger,
settling into it with less than her customary
grace.

Not much interrupted her sire, she reflected, when he had hunting on his pro-
gram. That he had gone so far as to check
the genetic pattern of the new Cavernus
emphasized his brief visit. Caissa knew
very well that Baythan had rejected several
exceptional intra-stellar contracts for her.
Yet, search her mind as deep as she could
for the reason behind this extraordinary
recommendation, she could find no valid

advantage to an heir-contract with the callow Cavernus Gustin.

Baythan's hint that he might culminate his Ministry on Demeathorn was even more startling. Whatever his mission was, it had drawn the High Lady Cinna of Aldebaran, Caissa's womb-mother, back to Demeathorn throughout Caissa's infancy and childhood. Ostensibly, the High Lady Cinna had contracted to oversee Caissa's early training and education.

Part of that training, which included intensive study of the involved contracts of FSP society — body-heir alliances, heir-contracts, host-child negotiations and other personal service treaties — suggested to Caissa that the heir-contract between her parents contained an undisclosed clause. Certainly the Lady Cinna had obliquely referred to contractual defaulters often enough in Baythan's presence.

The High Lady Cinna was governor-general of four of the wealthiest planets in the Federation yet she made time in the star-hopping life that she led to visit Caissa and Baythan to whom she had inexplicably remained contractually bound.

True, Baythan had an immaculate lineage, descending from the earliest of space pioneers, an excellent genetic pattern with few recessives. He was a skilled diplomatist, fearless hunter, deft lover, had impeccable taste in mundane matters of dress, design and art and, Caissa thought with objective detachment, was the most handsome man on Demeathorn. She knew that highly placed women frequently made the journey to Demeathorn for the sole purpose of conceiving their body-heir with him. Caissa's womb-mother, in a moment of rare intimacy, had remarked that, had she known Baythan before she had entered her own heir-contract, she might have conceived her first child by him as well.

It had become expedient in the twenty-second century for the wealthy and important men and women of the Federated Sentient Planets to ensure that their riches or hereditary positions remained in a direct, and genetically pure, blood line, secured in the person of one healthy heir-designate.

This heir had to be conceived naturally (by direct copulation) and be physically perfect at birth, surviving that event by at least three months, or the contract was considered void.

An intricate tattooed pattern of special inks that could not be duplicated ringed the neck of every body-heir, displayed as warning as well as defense. The child was inviolate and protected by the most stringent galactic laws and penalties, thereby eliminating blood feuds, kidnapping and the presumptive machinations of any greedy sibling of the same parent. Each man and woman had one body-heir, distinguished by the parent's tattoo. Of course, man or woman could produce additional children — (the wealthy woman generally employing a host-mother) and provide for them as they wished but the one body-heir enjoyed an incontestable position, zealously guarded, rigidly trained and especially instructed to increase the credit and holdings bequeathed to him or her. And to perpetuate the physical perfection which was as impor-

tant a prerequisite for the monied, titled and intelligent as their credit balance.

Once Caissa's physical perfection and health had been duly attested and Baythan had declared her his official body-heir and ordered her tattoo, he had provided a substantial income for her from investments and businesses on nine other worlds where he had shrewdly placed his own inherited capital during his various ministries for the Federated Planetary System. The High Lady Cinna had capriciously bestowed on her womb-daughter rich mineral rights from two planets and three moons.

Now twenty years old, Caissa knew that she should seriously consider supplying herself with an heir and, by custom, be guided by her sire's recommendations. Dutiful though she was to Baythan's few requests, Caissa could not in conscience consider any sort of alliance with the new Cavernus. Baythan had, however, invoked the recollection of a conversation and a subsequent painful incident with the High Lady Cinna six years ago, the day before Caissa's fourteenth birthday celebration, the day that Caissa had ventured to raise the matter of the private clause.

"So that I may know how to set out the most advantageous contracts and alliances for myself, Lady Cinna," Caissa had hastily explained as the Lady gave her an unexpectedly sharp appraisal.

"You must ask your noble sire about that clause." A slight, sly smile curled the Lady Cinna's delicately tinted lips. "He is in default and I have no wish to embarrass him."

Since the High Lady Cinna took an outrageous pleasure in doing just that as frequently as she could, Caissa maintained a bland look of inquiry.

"Be certain, my pet, to ask for the attainable in any negotiations." The Lady Cinna took up her hand mirror, checking her elaborate hair style — golden at this season of the year. "I unwisely erred, one of my few misjudgments. I took the promise for the deed, based on past accomplishments. Oh, I'm positive that your sire meant well and I thought coelura well worth waiting for. . . ."

"Coelura?"

"Yes, coelura," said Lady Cinna brusquely, adjusting a drape of the gossamer fabric that garbed her. "What else do you think distinguished this wretched little planet with its senescent troglodytes? Surely *you've* been told of coelura? Ah!" and the Lady Cinna exclaimed in arch comprehension. "No one at all then has mentioned coelura in your presence?" Her brittle laugh had made Caissa quiver. "I could well appreciate that certain data had been expunged from public information but, as your sire's body-heir, you ought to have been told."

Immediately after Caissa had been dismissed from Lady Cinna's presence, she had tried to remedy her ignorance. Data retrieval would give her no assistance until she obtained official clearance. That meant that there was information locked in the Blue City's memory banks. However, as she was also preparing for her fourteenth birthday celebration at which she achieved certain privileges and responsibilities, the urgency of acquiring forbidden knowledge was overshadowed. The day after that fabulous occasion, the Lady Cinna requested the pres-

ence of Baythan and Caissa and announced that she would leave Demeathorn within the hour.

"I have had more than sufficient of the company in your two pitiful Triadic Cities, and certainly more than enough of the hunting and fishing which is evidently all this trivial planet can now boast," she told Baythan with trenchant scorn. "Until *you* can fulfill *your* part of *your* contract, I shall return to my duties and obligations on other, better endowed worlds."

She had held that scornful smile, subtly goading Baythan to protest her accusation of failure but he had remained silent, grimly pale at her insult.

"And I suppose, failing all else, you will bequeath your quest to your heir," and the High Lady turned indolently to smile with arch sympathy on her offspring, "who will undoubtedly make a competent minister in your place, knowing the planet as well as she does and so sensibly conditioned for the existence here."

With a final scathing glance at her mute listeners, she swept from the room in a froth

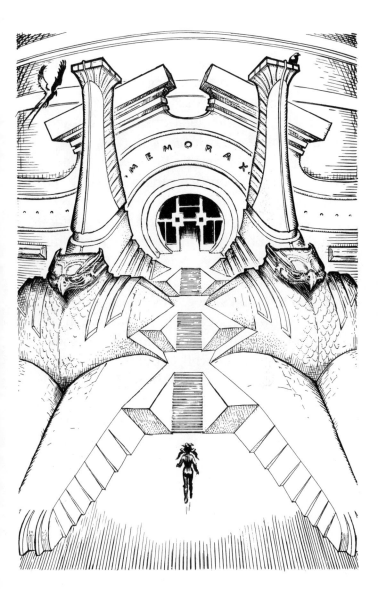

of fragrant fabric. Her denunciation of Bay-than made it impossible for Caissa, unwilling to remind her sire of that distressing scene, to raise the questions of the unmentioned clause or coelura.

Caissa could, and had, invoked her new rights as a fourteen year old body-heir to the classified section of Blue City's Memorax.

"Coelura," and the display printed reluctantly word by word instead of paragraphic speed, "a passive ovoid aerial life form once indigenous to the northeastern group of islands known as the Oriolis group."

Questioning "Oriolis," a name Caissa had not previously heard though she knew Demeathorn quite well, provided more perplexity and less information. The Oriolii were interdicted by the Triadic Council. For the first time in her carefully tutored life, Caissa recognized that "triad" meant three and she knew only two cities on Demeathorn, the Blue and the Red. Blue and red are primary colors.

"Yellow Triad City" elicited the information that there had been a third City, now abandoned. It had served as a trade and

COELURA · A PASSIVE AERIAL LIFE FORM ONCE INDIGENOUS TO THE NORTHERN GROUP OF ISLANDS KNOWN AS THE ORIOLIS GROUP.

export center for a product no longer available. Yellow Triad City had been put on minimal care one hundred and twenty years ago. An update line informed Caissa that the ruins were now considered dangerous even for protected excursions.

Summoning a geographic display of Demeathorn's large, roughly triangular continent, Caissa regarded it thoughtfully. Blue Triad City was in the southeastern corner, enjoying quite the best temperature on its plateau. Red Triad City was in a direct line of flight to the southwest, situated on the vast bluff that shoved into the western sea. If one considered an equilateral triangle, the upper tip would put the abandoned city precisely north, again in an elevated position, overlooking the scattering of islands that staggered northwards, presumably the interdicted Oriolis group.

Further queries, even using her father's private code, brought discouraging answers that were in their phrasing subtle evasions. No sporting animals, no facilities, interdiction by the Red and Blue rulers for residents

RED TRIAD
CITY

or visitors due to extreme hazards and lack of rescue units.

Caissa made a rapid calculation which confirmed that the range of any of the rescue vehicles serving the sporting and fishing areas could reach the farthest north island at a push, even if they had to rely on solar-charged batteries for a return flight. She could extract nothing further about coelura which, in her mother's estimation, had distinguished Demeathorn and which once had generated the need for the third city. Even at fourteen, Caissa had deduced that much.

She had abandoned such fruitless research though occasionally in the first few months, she had tried alternative questions on the Memorax. Then she had begun to participate actively in the sporting life which absorbed her sire, and occupied the planet's inhabitants and the many visitors who came to enjoy hunting Demeathorn's canny, deadly and diverse predators.

The intervening six years had passed pleasantly enough for Caissa and she acquired the status of "quota hunter," no small achievement. She had a reputation as well as private wealth to pass on to her own body-heir. Now, mulling over her sire's request that she consider the new Cavernus, she wondered how that could be connected with Baythan's boast that he would, at long last, accomplish his mysterious mission and restore his contractual honor with the High Lady Cinna. Caissa would willingly have supported her sire in any effort to acquit himself with the High Lady, but marrying that insipid Cavernus was stretching the sire-bond very thin indeed.

Caissa rose to pace restlessly about the reception room, reviewing heir-contracts and intimacy requirements. "A small sacrifice today that might reap unexpected rewards," Baythan had said. "I took the promise for the deed," Lady Cinna's high pure voice reminded her.

Although it had been six years ago that the High Lady had officially left Demeathorn, she had made sporadic and unannounced visits to the Blue Triadic City in which Baythan and Caissa resided. Aware of the antagonism between her natural par-

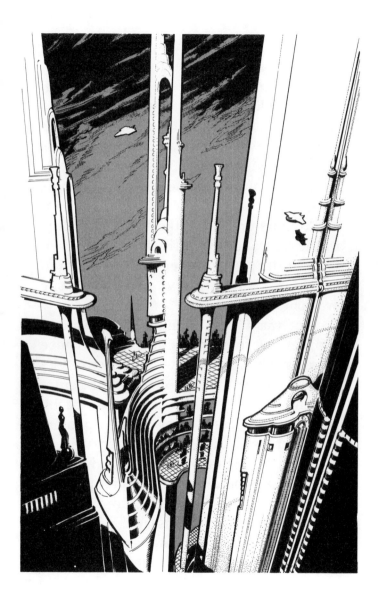

ents, Caissa noticed that these visits invariably occurred when her sire was protocologically unable to disappear on a hunt or some ministerial errand. Very privately, Caissa likened the Lady Cinna's attitude towards Baythan as similar to the sly, six-legged deadly nathus of Demeathorn's deep forests, a creature of immense patience for stalking its prey from the aerial advantage of the closely grown ferfa trees. Her father, on the other hand, reacted like a man caught in a labyrinth, trying to find the one way out to the sun.

Nor was Caissa immune to her womb-mother's verbal pricks and darts. These were mainly concerned with the lack of "elegant or suitable" males to carry on the quintessential qualities of Caissa's historically illustrious heritage of governors, explorers spatial and scientific, male and female.

Though Baythan had full custody of his heir, Caissa could have requested permission to go anywhere in the galaxy that her private income, which was large, permitted. The Lady Cinna had, however, prejudiced herself in her natural daughter's estimation

by humiliating the sire in the heir's presence. In the strict terms of contracts which Caissa had studied, as long as Baythan lived, he could not be held in default of that unpublished clause. A strange condition, indeed, Caissa thought, if, as his heir, she would inherit the obligation.

But Caissa had not wished to travel from Demeathorn, certainly not in the exalted Lady Cinna's company, for she didn't much like the woman's ruthlessness, brittle ways and excessive devotion to bizarre fashions, often including body changes. If such practices were essential for social acceptance outside Demeathorn's system, Caissa preferred to stay with her father. Again, being candid, Caissa had lately become bored with a life totally devoted to days spent in hunting parties and evenings in parties discussing the days' hunts.

The previous spring, Caissa had been tempted to travel to another system and had asked her sire's permission.

"Travel? You've just got back from a visit to Red City. Oh, you mean star travel!" Baythan had regarded his heir thoughtfully. "She's been nagging at you, has she?"

"Not recently," Caissa had truthfully replied.

"For all of me, you can go wherever you wish. Although the karnsore season is about to start. You haven't forgotten your wager with Rhondus of Rigel Four, have you?"

"Certainly not."

Baythan had smiled as he gave her shoulder a paternal pat. "Good girl. Then go *after* the karnsore season. Do you good. Get your quota hunter status on different worlds. It sharpens the instincts."

During the excitement of that spectacular karnsore hunt and her triumph over Rhondus by three kills, Caissa forgot her half-formed resolve to travel. Rhondus had been a good loser, as befit his rank, and had invited her to join him in a hunt on his native planet. As Rigel Four was in the Lady Cinna's sphere of dominance, Caissa had pleaded duties which kept her on Demea-thorn and tactfully introduced Rhondus to a Caverna with short-term contracts on her mind.

Caissa had been very surprised when the next ministerial courier had brought her a cascade of magnificent, perfectly matched firegems. In a handwritten note, itself an unusual mark of favor for a womb-child who had disappointed her dam, Lady Cinna advised Caissa to choose only a man who could out-hunt her.

Caissa had chosen to be amused by the sly insult. Now, with Baythan promoting an heir-contract with a Cavernus who only hunted in caverns well enough lit to take full advantage of photophobic prey or rode after the fleet but timid rerbok, the High Lady Cinna's taunt rankled.

Hunting? Baythan had been dressed for hunting and he had not suggested that she join him. Caissa was alarmed. That could mean that the new Cavernus was already in the Blue City, had approached Baythan personally and probably been encouraged by her sire for that unspecified reason of reward.

"Trin," Caissa called out, running to her

dressing room as she stripped off her wrap, "dress me quickly. The new Cavernus may be making a call."

A fleeting look of surprise crossed the old dresser's face to be replaced instantly by the appropriately intent expression of the devoted personal servant.

As she was being suitably arrayed in semi-formal morning attire, Caissa found time to run a computer check on the new Cavernus's public credit and property, hoping to find something positive about the applicant. Exact figures were not available without special coding but it was obvious that the Diolla Mines of Gustin's inheritance produced a steady profit, the domestic satisfaction of his tenants and free miners was excellent and his assessed private wealth included valuable mining sites on two of Demeathorn's four moons and active drilling in domed compounds on three methane atmosphere planets in nearby systems. She could extract a fine endowment in an heir-contract — if she could only stomach the sire.

Trin had just finished winding green

ocean stones into Caissa's long, naturally black, plaited hair when Gustin's arrival at her reception entrance was flashed on the screen of her inner chamber.

Depressing the release toggle, Caissa welcomed Gustin, keeping her words formal as she invited him to enter. He had come, she noticed as he stepped within range of the visuals in the reception room, properly garbed for someone wanting to negotiate an heir-contract. He carried a gift casket.

Caissa let him wait, observing with inner satisfaction his nervous pace, the occasional twitch he gave to settle the drape of a tunic which did not hide the fact that his shoulders required some padding. He was a shade knock-kneed and his calves in their ceremonial laces wanted more muscle before they'd display to advantage. Gustin was, as most young nobles, handsome of face and, aside from those minor deficiencies of shoulder-breadth and leg, well proportioned. What did not match his appearance was his mind, Caissa thought with a sigh.

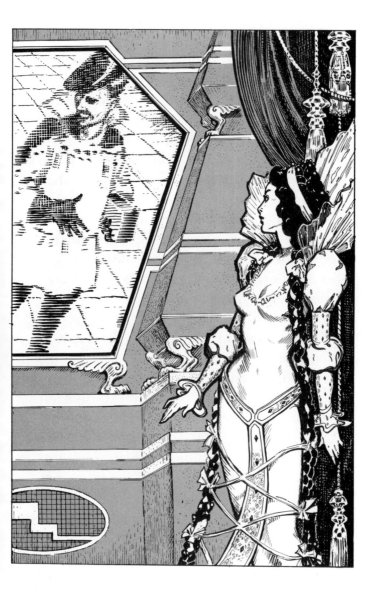

As she swept out to meet the suitor, Caissa reminded herself that her duty to her sire required her to consider his wishes, to remember that an heir-contract was limited to the conception, gestation and bearing of one live healthy child, and that her sire had intimated that a contract with a Cavernus right now would have a reward.

Exactly three-quarters of an hour later, Caissa, dressed for hunting, was making good speed in the fast lane of the Blue City's internal grav channels towards the perimeter hangar where she kept her speedster. She cursed under her breath, using the more pungent cavern miners' dialect to vent her fury.

Gustin, having misinterpreted Baythan's hurry to go hunting with ratification of his suit, had achieved new heights of fatuity. His initial greeting indicated to Caissa that he took it for granted that any woman would be delighted to gestate his body-heir now that he was Cavernus. He had shoved the gift casket at her, running on about the wealth and comfort of his home Cavern as though his familial estate was vastly superi-

or to apartments in the Blue City. Caissa had tried, without success, to interrupt his catalog of the benefits of instant promotion to Caverna. She had tried to point out that this was only an initial meeting, that nothing was by any means settled and no contract terms established. He even opened the casket himself, to show her bluestones, generally proffered for minor contracts, but to compound that insult, the jewels had apparently been cut and polished by a rank apprentice and were set in poorly etched platinum.

The combination of obtuseness and presumption on his part made Caissa lose her temper. Restraining the urge to throw the paltry gift in his face, she had pushed the casket against his diaphragm with such vigor that his hands came up in a protective gesture. She relinquished her hold so abruptly that he stumbled, trying not to drop the box. She then informed him in explicit terms that his manners would have put his humblest miner to shame, that he was pretentious, miserly, impertinent and ultimately the last man on Demeathorn with whom she would consider a contract of any sort, much less one requiring the intimacy of conceiving an heir.

She had left him standing, gape-mouthed, in the center of the reception room, still clutching the casket to his midriff. She was no sooner past the inner door than she had triggered the holdfast. She called for Trin to bring her hunting gear, unfastening her formal clothes, stepping away from the fallen garments and into the ones Trin hurriedly tendered.

She reached the hangar level in record time, seething when she found her slim speedster blocked by other craft. One of the privileges of being the heir of a Minister Plenipotential was that Caissa ranked just below the Triadic heirs and above Cavernii. She also had more freedom to come and go from the Triadic Cities without undue interference by the Guardians. Out of courtesy she dialed her exit request through to Blue Guardian and then ordered hangar attendants to move the vehicles blocking hers. Inside the cabin of the fast vehicle, she contacted Blue City Control for clearance.

"Just going out for a spin," she told the Guardian on duty. "To watch my sire bring in his hunt."

"Now that may not be so easy, Lady Caissa," the Guardian began, surprise and concern flashing across his stolid countenance.

He was a nice old man, in his thirteenth decade, and had taught Caissa much about the dangers of inner and outer Demeathorn. A teaching, she thought now, that he might regret since she had so well displayed herself capable of handling most of the dangerous species on the planet — including the ones from which to retreat without loss of dignity — that he could summon little reason to deny her egress. "Your sire gave no specific directions for his hunt. . . ."

"Oh, that's all right, Guardian. . . ."

"Lady Caissa . . ."

"Thank you, Guardian," and she snapped off the channel.

He flashed an urgent request to speak with her again but she was not in a mood to hear advice or admonition. She took a northwesterly route, low along the moun-

tain ridges where transmissions would be
jammed. She accelerated to the top speed of
her vehicle so that the dangers of low level
flying exhilarated her and demanded total
concentration. She was not a reckless driver
by nature but the distasteful interview with
the fatuous Cavernus, her sire's unexpected
recommendation of the contract and the
well-remembered shafts of the High Lady
Cinna all combined to cause Caissa to dis-
card habit and, indeed, common sense.

Now and then her speedster flushed
game with its side-shadow. Once or twice
she changed direction to identify the creature. She had no heart for hunting, nor for
company. Then she wondered if she'd've
done better to seek out some of the gay,
effervescent, frivolous companions, either
City or Cavern, and forget in laughter and
society the doubts that plagued her.

She turned north again, to keep the
coast range between herself and the Blue
City transmissions. Her thoughts turned
back continuously, not to the Cavernus Gustin, but to her father's hope of fulfilling his
mission. Whatever it was. She tried to recall

with whom her sire had lately been keeping company, with whom he'd been hunting, even what his catch had been and she couldn't call up a single detail. When he'd say that his hunting had been good that day, she'd conventionally offered congratulations and let the matter drop. Baythan had never been braggart of head, horn or hatch. Now that she reviewed their infrequent recent exchanges, it was singularly odd of Baythan not to have stated where or with whom he had hunted.

But, if Baythan were at the point of fulfilling his mission as well as his contract clause with the Lady Cinna, what did that have to do with hunting?

Suddenly she caught the sparkle and flash of maneuvering aircraft in the west. She veered seaward, preventing casual observation of her vehicle. She skimmed the rough ocean, watching as huge amphibians launched themselves at her ship's shadow, flailing with fluke and tentacle. She adjusted her speedster's altitude for she'd hunted these waters enough to know the

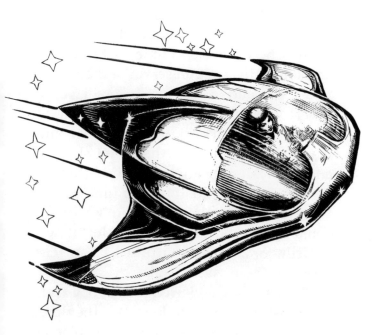

dangers. When the coast curved slightly northwest, she continued straight. She wanted no chance encounter with hunters and one of the best preserves of the nathus was just inland.

No "reward" she could possibly imagine would be worth accepting physical intimacy with Gustin. On that point she was adamant. But, if an alliance with a Cavernus was advisable at this point in time, surely there must be another noble with whom she could form a short term treaty. Must it necessarily, for Baythan's purposes, be an heir-contract?

Mentally she reviewed the list of Cavernii, most of whom she knew for they preferred smaller residences in either Blue or Red City to their spacious subterranean holdings. "Home" did not, Caissa had been informed by one Caverna, apply to caverns: they could be made comfortable enough and suitably adapted to miners' and artisans' need, but were not in the least "home-like." Caissa had found the enormous caverns which riddled Demeathorn's coastal mountains rather fascinating. Or, at least,

the hunting in them. As living quarters, she did indeed prefer the sweeping prospect from her windows in the upper levels of Blue City.

Triad city. And there were three. Whimsically, Caissa altered her course for that abandoned third city. She might as well have some goal in her flight, preferably where she would be least expected. Yellow Triad City, ruins and all, beckoned.

A sudden drop and an ominous wobble in her speedster's flight brought her forcibly to attention. And she was in difficulties. For the first time in her life, she had failed to check the fuel tanks and the remaining supply would not take her much farther. The sun was too far west now for her to recharge her auxiliary solar batteries though they contained enough to maintain shielding and life support within the speedster overnight.

She changed direction towards the distant shore and checked her position. She wasn't far from the Yellow City on a north heading but if the place was abandoned, nocturnal predators would be abundant

and dangerous. She checked for the proximity of habitable caverns and the initial display gave her none. As the entire perimeter of the continent was a maze of caverns, she keyed an emergency override and, after a significant pause, the display informed her that she was headed for the Oriolii caverns which were interdicted. Well, she couldn't expect help from them with her speedster emblazoned with both Blue Triad and ministerial markings.

Caissa was annoyed with herself for failing to check her fuel reserves. Perhaps that was what the Guardian had tried to tell her when she switched him off. Not that she couldn't be safe enough in the speedster overnight: its plastisteel body was impervious to anything except ressor acid. Those creatures dwelt near mountain lakes, lurking in forests between forays into caverns. She need only find a suitably open rocky area, preferably away from dense vegetation in which a carnivore might secrete itself. In the morning, the sun would recharge the auxiliaries sufficiently for her to return to Blue City at a judicious speed.

The jagged rocks of the coastline were now visible. Nearer loomed rocky extrusions that must be off-shore islands. An extensive one appeared on her scope.

She opened a channel now to report her position to Blue City Tower and realized two problems: one, she was too far from any Triadic receiver to report on the power she had left; second, a faint emergency sequence disrupted the regular channel configuration. She tuned as finely as she could but the sequence remained faint, not with the irregularity of distance but lack of power. Swiftly she cut in the locator and her concern deepened. The distress call emanated from a point not far to her right on the large island. She swung the speedster towards it, locking into the thread of sound and approaching as fast as she dared once she was over the island's forested and rough terrain.

She skipped over the rocky bastion, down into the valley it protected from the sea. A sun-struck dazzle caught her eye on the northeastern end. Then she observed the swath cut from the treetops and climb-

ing vines though rapid growth had re-
moved the seared vegetation. She slowed
forward motion as she reached the valley's
far side. Then she saw the crashed vehicle.
It was of obsolete design and she wondered
how it had remained airborne at all. It had
skidded across the first low ridge, losing its
guidance vanes, and had dropped into a
gully beyond the ridge, its nose half buried
in the inland rim of the island's bastion ring.
Caissa wondered that anyone could have
survived such a crash but the emergency
signal, faint though it was, argued that
someone had.

This might be an island in the interdicted Oriolis group, but no one refused to
answer a distress call.

Slowly she circled the ridge and gully
and found, not far from the crash, a narrow
ledge which would accommodate her
speedster. Nothing could come at it from
the bare rock on the island side and there
was no cover at all on the cliff looming
above.

She tapped out a contingency code for
her speedster in case she encountered diffi-

culties. The craft, once its batteries were charged in the morning, was programmed with her precise location and would return to Blue Triad on automatic if she did not reset it.

Caissa donned a tough coverall, prepared herself with hand and thigh weapons, emergency medical and food supplies, survival kit and pack.

Before she could close the canopy behind her, the sky above her head erupted into a flight of rainbows, spinning rather than flying. Round rainbows that sang a liquid and lovely welcome for she couldn't construe that glorious sound into menace of any kind. Standing motionless, she whistled back at them, trying to reproduce several of the notes of the thousands sung at her. An hilarious response, delighted laughter, greeted her poor effort and she laughed back in pure joy. Whatever the darting creatures were, they meant her no harm. They wheeled and veered and, Caissa thought, seemed to be urging her towards the eastern side of the ridge, away from the crash.

She felt compelled to follow them, their happy exultation overwhelming her original purpose in landing. They led her quickly to an unexpected break in the island's palisade. A section of the basalt had fallen from the escarpment, creating a steep slope down to the edge of a little lagoon where the larger boulders formed an uneven horn into the water. The sea was burnished bronze, with the palette of the setting sun marking out jutting tips of other basaltic debris beyond the sheltered beach.

The rainbow creatures deserted her abruptly. Then she saw them congregate by the edge of the lagoon, by the black boulders. To her astonishment she saw a man rise from the water and stare in her direction. She waved to reassure him, mildly astonished that he did not exhibit more enthusiasm at her arrival, however long overdue his rescue might be. She made additional broad gestures of friendship and aid that could not be misunderstood.

In doing so, she lost her footing on the slithery gap, slid unceremoniously and bruisingly down the slope to the beach. The

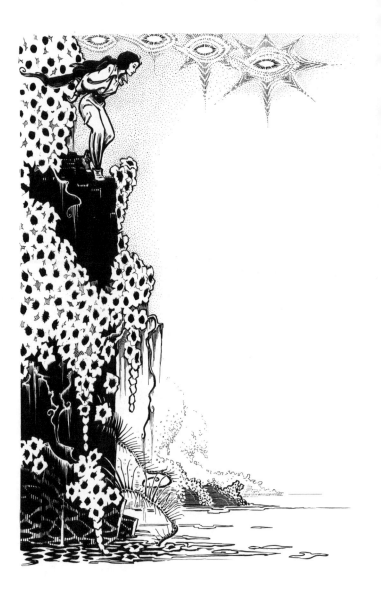

rescuer rescued? She had regained her feet and her composure when the man made his own way out of the water. He might not have seen her ignominious descent. Only then did she notice that his right arm was crooked and he dragged his right leg.

She was momentarily stunned for physical injuries were quickly corrected and deformities simply unknown. She sternly reminded herself that he had been in a crash, had had no surgical treatment to mend injuries sustained weeks before and she must be discreet and tolerant.

Then the man whistled in an incredibly complex glissando. The voluble round aerial creatures smothered him in iridescent strands. In a matter of seconds, they flitted away and he was clad in the most gorgeous raiment she had ever seen, his unsightly injuries masked.

"Coelura, a passive ovoid indigenous life form." That hard-won data flashed through Caissa's mind. Coelura! The only thing that distinguished Demeathorn! Fashion was of major importance to the High Lady Cinna.

She would have prized as invaluable the garment the man now wore.

Coelura, spinning iridescent garments, had been the product of the Yellow Triad City. And was coelura the reason the Oriolis had been expelled from the Triadic Cities? Why? Snippets of information began to mesh. She had assumed that coelura were no longer available. Could this island flock be all that remained? Was her sire's mission to rediscover coelura? With bitter certainty, Caissa knew that a coelura garment would satisfy that unfulfilled clause in Baythan's heir-contract with the High Lady Cinna.

Caissa was seized suddenly with an anguish so cruel and a rage so deep that she nearly burst into tears. Baythan had sounded so positive of success. If he knew of coelura, how *could* he put such joyous creatures in jeopardy to the fashion-hunger of the galaxy?

Coelura trilled her a reassurance which eased that stabbing, unfilial accusation. They swirled ecstatically about the man they had clothed in splendor. In splendor, and more, for now he was close enough for her to distinguish that other difference about him. Crippled he might be, walking slowly to disguise a halting stride, but in his face, handsome in feature, was a serenity, a self-awareness that she had never before observed in any of her acquaintance.

Some heretofore unexperienced compulsion caused her to extend her arms forward, palms up, in respectful greeting. She smiled, a smile as warm and genuine as his, totally unprompted by propriety or protocol.

"You survived that dreadful crash!" she said, wondering how anyone in his present state could be as happy as he.

"Barely," he replied, indicating by a slight nod of his head the damaged side of his body.

"Your signal was so very faint that I despaired of finding anyone alive."

"The signal, my lady, has been on for so long I had despaired of its being heard at all."

He clasped her hands as equal to equal as naturally as if they had met under formal conditions. The faintest squeeze of his-

strong left hand emphasized the irony of his words.

"You didn't expect to be rescued at all?" Inadvertently her eyes went to his throat which the high-necked gown covered.

"I am now found."

Her ear caught the note in his voice that augured ill for those who had not searched until they found him. Or perhaps he was not, as she had assumed by his manner, a body-heir.

"I have been considering the construction of a boat to take me back to the mainland. My absence might precipitate matters. Would your vehicle possibly carry two?"

"Of course . . . but not now."

"Oh?"

Caissa cleared her throat, aware of his amusement at her hesitation.

"I neglected to check my fuel tanks before leaving Blue City . . ." and, when he smiled kindly at such a lapse, she went on purposefully. "My own fault but I had not intended to come so far and then heard your distress signal."

"How far will the remainder of your fuel

take you?" His expression became concerned and the flowing blue-green of his robe turned grey.

"By tomorrow, when the solar batteries have charged, I can transport you anywhere you wish."

"Even to interdicted territory?"

"Rescue missions are exempt."

His smile deepened and his robe brightened, too.

"And how do you explain your overnight absence to the Blue City Guardians?"

"With any plausible story I care to concoct on my way back," she replied with a shrug and a smile to belie a callous indifference to truth and authority. "Do not worry on my account. I am only pleased to restore you." She faltered then, feeling a blush suffuse her face as if she were an undisciplined adolescent for she was not conducting his rescue in a proper way. "I brought my medical kit," she added, reaching for it.

"I'm long past the need, dear lady. The coelura eased my pain as they also sheltered and provided for me."

Anguish again stabbed Caissa.

"Then they are coelura!"

"They are indeed!" The quality of his voice cooled and, though his face remained serene, she felt him grow stern and his gown rippled darker.

"I've only heard of coelura once," she said, swallowing.

"Once is usually enough." His sternness was disconcerting.

"What I heard did not lead me to suspect their existence or . . ." and she glanced above her at the glorious spinning coelura who were murmuring lightly, but without alarm.

"What did you hear?" The man was polite if adamant.

Seized by a sudden whim, she replied, mimicking the voice of a computer. " 'Coelura, a passive ovoid aerial life form once indigenous to the northeastern Oriolis island group.' That was all."

"And 'Oriolis'?" the man prompted.

" 'Oriolii have been interdicted by the Triadic cities and no intercourse is permitted.' "

"Yet you deviated from your course to

answer a survivor signal in an interdicted area?"

"A survivor signal is not to be ignored from whatever source," she replied with mock reproval.

The man laughed, an easy, hearty sound, unlike the artificial and socially acceptable snickers of her society.

Suddenly the coelura massed together, uttering a trill that was a warning despite its melodiousness.

"Come, we must hurry," said the man. "The sun is setting. While the coelura are abroad, we are safe. Once the sun is set, they rest and nocturnal amphibians prowl this beach. I have a shelter, rude but sufficient, a short . . . hop . . . from here."

"But there are reasons why . . ." Caissa began, thinking unfilial thoughts about her sire's possible involvement in this man's accident. She was torn between a desire to detach herself completely and a deeper, burgeoning fear for the fate of the coelura if her sire's stratagems were successful.

"*There* are more urgent reasons why you will obey me," said the man, pointing towards the undulating shapes that were speeding across the lagoon towards the shore. "The prinas are wasting no time. They have our scent."

Caissa required no further admonition as he took her hand and pulled her towards the thick vegetation just beyond the beach. Prinas were as fast on land as they were in the water.

"The coelura will mask our spoor. But we must hurry."

"I thought coelura were passive," she said, deftly pushing back the thick growth at her host's right side. Coelura swirled behind them, their collective voice now almost menacing.

"You mustn't believe everything you see displayed, my lady. Coelura are generally the most obliging creatures in the world but they also recognize danger."

Then they had reached his shelter, built against the base of the basaltic palisade. The sloping roof was only apparent because the flight of coelura settled on its outline. Caissa couldn't imagine what had been used in its construction.

The man stepped to an apparently seam-
less wall and pulled open a doorway. She
quickly entered and, as he followed her, the
entrance sealed itself.

"I would scarcely call this shelter rude,"
Caissa said, staring about her appreciative-
ly.

The single unexpectedly large room was
decorated, if not furnished, in patterns that
glowed of themselves. The rock of the back
wall was covered with shimmering strands.
Natural stone formations had been trans-
formed into a long couch. Other rock extrusions served as shelving for bowls of fruit, a
leaf-covered plate and gourds.

"This is a beautiful place."

"And you naturally have been taught to
appreciate beauty?"

She gave him a sharp look for the odd
flatness in his voice.

"I have been so trained but . . ." and she
gestured about her as the patterns of the
very fabric of the room seemed to shift and
flow subtly, "but this transcends that over-
used word."

"Rude or beauty?"

"You are rude," she replied stiffly, "who are clothed in beauty."

He smiled then, as if he had been testing her, and his smile reached blue eyes accentuated by the greeny-blue of his gown.

"My apologies. I have been long away from graciousness."

"Living here?"

"Living alone. And here."

The care in which he phrased that qualification did not escape her even if she did not comprehend the distinction.

"May I offer you juice, or water?" He was the easy, courteous host after that curious exchange. "While the coelura supply my needs, the fare is primitive." He gestured with his uninjured arm for her to seat herself on the long couch.

On the horns of her private dilemma, Caissa hesitated. To offer hospitality signified her host's good intentions: for her to accept bound her as well. If her suspicion about Baythan's ambition was correct, she might be in danger of violating that mutual trust.

"Not the sort of fare to which you are

accustomed . . ." and his gaze turned mocking as his garb altered color.

"It's not that, truly." Suddenly Caissa wanted this man's good opinion more than she wished to violate the ethics of hospitality. "I often eat from the land when I hunt." To cover her confusion, she reached to a thigh pocket and withdrew the emergency rations. "I have these to contribute to our meal. Perhaps a change to your diet." She held the package tactfully towards his left hand.

Once more he laughed in his spontaneous and infectious manner and took her offering.

"I *have* lived alone too long, my lady." He moved towards the shelves, taking down the fruit bowl and placing it on the center of the couch. "Make yourself comfortable. That protective coverall is no longer necessary and it must be hot."

Caissa was finding it so and, as the man unwrapped the rations and soaked the dehydrated portions in a small bowl, she took off the coverall and seated herself on the couch.

Having expected stone, she found the surface comfortably yielding. Curious, she touched the fabric covering. It was remarkably soft yet firm, and she found herself stroking it as if it were the pelt of some creature domesticated for tactility.

"Is this also coelura spun?" she asked.

She sensed his sudden wariness and then noticed that his eyes were on her throat and the body-heir tattoo.

"Ah, I had expected as much," he said, unaccountably relaxing. "Your bearing is unmistakable."

Offended, she started to rise but he gave her a broad mischievous grin and thrust a plate at her.

"You're not what I would have expected for one of your status. Here, these are bark peelings which the coelura collect for me. Exceedingly nutritious for one who has had a trying day." His eyes were kind and his manner so conciliatory she could not remain resentful.

He positioned the rest of their meal beside the fruit and gestured elegantly with his left hand for her to be seated again.

"My name is Murell, my lady."

"Mine is Caissa."

They smiled at each other for the belatedness of that formality as they sat down.

"And yes, my lady Caissa, this is coelura spun and the shelter is coelura fabricated. They sometimes use extraneous materials in their constructions. There was a time," and his face lost its mobility, "when men and women paid enormous fortunes to Demeathorn for coelura spins. One sufficed for the lifetime of even the most devotedly fashionable."

Caissa bent her head as if to select food but she could not look at Murell, thinking as she was of the studied elegance of her mother's extensive, ever-changing wardrobe.

"Each coelura," Murell went on, unaware of her internal conflict, "has only so much thread in its life span. They are willing creatures, eager to please those they like. Unfortunately, they are pliant and amiable to almost anyone. . . ."

"They don't like prinas. . . ."

"Prinas are natural predators, indigenous to this planet." Murell spoke in a wry tone and Caissa, dressed for hunting, knew all too well that man was the most insatiable predator of the galaxy.

"Coelura must reserve some thread with which to construct its mating net, a net which was considered by the connoisseur to be more valuable than ordinary thread."

Caissa saw the color of his gown turning granitic and as cold as the tone of his voice. She dared not look at him, suppressing her own roiling anxieties, inexplicably convinced that he, or his coelura spun gown, would sense her increasing fear. A fear that had more to do with the continued protection of coelura from her sire's plans than betraying their presence to anyone.

"The Oriolis *left* the Triad to prevent coelura extinction?" she asked in the composed tone that only years of training could produce under this evening's circumstances.

"I have offered you hospitality, Caissa." Murell's voice was unaccountably gentle as if he knew the direction her thoughts were taking.

"And I have accepted." Despite all her discipline, Caissa could not suppress the anguish she experienced at her invidious situation. Suddenly the fabric under her began to wrap itself about her legs but the ripple was reassuring, not aggressive. She stared down at the phenomenon of affectionate fabric.

"Stop that," said Murell in an authoritative voice.

Startled, she looked up at him but he was staring at the couch. His command was directed at the covering. The material resumed its former quiescence. Then Murell's eyes met hers.

"You are a body-heir, Caissa. We have shared hospitality. You have come to my rescue." His quiet words reminded her of duty and tradition, of unwritten laws of conduct and exchange of life-debts.

"Coelura is at risk right now." She tried to formulate a warning that would not violate her filial obligation.

"Coelura has been at risk and no longer is." Murell stated this, so quietly vehement that she was bereft of all politic phrases. He touched her hand gently. "Once you have put me back on the mainland, all will be well. Not to mince words, your fortuitous arrival will seal coelura's protection."

Whatever she might have been tempted to say in as direct speech as he had used was drowned by a savage shrieking howl. The fabric of the shelter's outer wall was dinted inward by a large body. Caissa was on her feet in an instant, reaching for the weapons hanging from her discarded coverall.

"Don't worry," Murell said, smiling at her alert reaction. "The amphibian cannot pierce coelura-built walls."

The creature attacked again and Caissa positioned herself before Murell, knowing that his injuries made movement awkward.

"I really do appreciate your effort, my dear Caissa," and Murell sounded oddly amused, "but weapons are unnecessary." He emitted a piercing whistle.

The creature outside snarled, more in pain than in anticipation. Murell repeated his whistle in a different and complex sequence. The sound was taken up all around them, the outer walls turning a brilliant purply-red as if emanating heat, though Caissa felt no increase in the temperature of the room. The attacker's shrieks turned to agonized whines and its noise dwindled as it put distance between itself and the source of its discomfort.

"Stop that," Murell said, once more in that authoritative voice.

Caissa swung back to him, immeasurably offended, and then saw that he was once again addressing whimsical coelura. The full skirts of his robe, now a purplish blue, had managed to wrap around her leg and tugged her gently towards Murell.

She caught his eyes and he gave her an embarrassed smile, snatching the fondling fold from her.

Caissa giggled. Her hands, which had tensed into flat defensive positions, went to her lips in a gesture reminiscent of her childhood. But the stresses of the last hour needed release and she had never been given to tears. At the sound of her irrepressible mirth, Murell, too, relaxed, his rich chuckle breaking into full laughter as dignity was forgotten.

Afterwards, Caissa supposed that she had clung to Murell as the excess of amusement overtook them. Somehow, his injured arm was not awkward as he held her to him, nor did she object in any way to being in his arms. He was exactly the right height for her. She laid her head gratefully against his shoulder, which needed no padding. She felt his cheek resting easily against her head as the embrace was extended long past the need of mutual support.

This time, as the robe enveloped her, Murell did not protest. Then, in an abrupt motion, he released her, stepping back, the fabric in danger of being torn by his energetic retreat.

"My apologies, Caissa," he said stiffly.

"No apologies are needed." She held herself proudly, hurt by his sudden rejection. But the hem of his gown reached towards her.

"Caissa," and he seemed to be arguing against himself to judge by the action and the conflict of color in his robe, "whatever attraction you might have just felt for me, might be emotionally experiencing, is

caused by proximity to coelura attuned to my needs. . . ." He broke off, his face and robe flushing with embarrassment.

"Well, coelura, and presumably you, have succeeded! You have made an honorable disclosure of intent. I am not averse to it. Now *do* something!"

"Not in this treacherous robe," he cried and ducked from under its folds, though how he accomplished such a maneuver, she didn't then understand. By the time his hands were removing her garments, the light in the shelter was dimming. She did see the narrow tattooed bands on his neck as she willingly sank to the delicious abandon of the waiting coelura couch.

Sunlight suffused the shelter when Caissa awoke languidly the next day. Coelura trilled a reassurance as she sat up and the covering lapped itself caressingly about her. Murell was nowhere in sight, though the entrance stood wide open.

She dressed quickly, despite the initial problem of disengaging herself from the bedcover. She must leave! She must take

Murell to the mainland. Then she must speed back to Blue Triad City, compose her confused thoughts and frustrated hopes, far away from the insidious and seductive atmosphere of coelura . . . and sadly, from Murell whom she must also forget. No, she doubted that she would ever *forget* this brief alliance. It would serve as a standard against which to measure some other man. If such as Murell could be found, for he had been man enough for her!

Profoundly she regretted the pressures that must separate them so quickly. She regretted the diverse circumstances that would prevent any future encounter.

She had just scooped the coverall from the floor when shadows crossed the doorway. Coelura trilled and their joy made her smile poignantly. Murell stood in the entrance, his grey-blue coelura now fitting tightly against his body. She knew before he spoke that he had been checking her speedster.

"The batteries are fully charged," he said in a slow deep voice that showed the regret as much as his garment did. "With that power and what you have in your fuel tanks, you should reach the base of the Triangle."

"Thank you, Murell," she said, putting as much and as little meaning as she could in that trite phrase. Then quickly she walked past him into the sun-dappled forest.

As they climbed slowly up to her speedster, for the path the coelura had found for Murell wound in steep but manageable gradients, the aerial rainbows encouraged them with trills and whistles. Their song seemed to be aimed at Caissa, trying to lighten her spirits. She wished that somehow there could be a more joyous conclusion for herself, Murell and Murell's faithful coelura. But they, above all, and he for whatever reason, must be protected by her silence.

Fortunately, he had to sit behind her in the speedster, there being but one pilot's seat. She concentrated on her flying and the directions he gave in a composed voice. She could feel his presence in every pore of her skin. She tried to discount this tremendous attraction for him to the coelura he wore but somehow . . .

He gave her a heading due east of the island and then pointed out the shoreline features where she was to turn inland. She marked one hundred kilometers in silence until he asked her to reduce altitude. The landing site was visible as a rocklined square in the midst of tossing vegetation that pushed against rocky upthrusts of what had once been one of Demeathorn's myriad volcanoes. She landed. She released the doorlock. He covered her hand with his.

"Go safely, Caissa. Be well!" His deep voice was charged with emotion. He stepped down, with an awkwardness that now endeared her last vision of him.

It was then that she realized no coelura were in evidence, dancing about him. She couldn't question that. Lifting the speedster to leave Murell was the hardest task she had ever performed. She did catch a final glimpse of him ducking into the jungle, the colorlessness of his clothes reflecting his regret at leaving her more than the most polished phrase.

*   *   *

When she was well within range, she contacted Blue City Tower, a smooth explanation of malfunction ready for the Chief Guardian. He responded by advising her of heavy air traffic into Blue Triad City and that she must surrender manual operation within sixty kilometers of the Tower. So, she hadn't even been missed. She could easily have remained with Murell a few days. . . . She abruptly cancelled such thoughts. No one must ever suspect that she had been northeast or anywhere near the interdicted Oriolis shores.

Trin had missed her and been keenly worried, Caissa discovered when she finally reached her apartments through the crowded grav channels.

"What's going on, Trin?" Caissa demanded. "No, I'm perfectly all right. I forgot to check my fuel tanks yesterday and had to wait until the batteries recharged this morning. I was completely safe from harm. Now, what is causing such furor? Cavernii seem to be assembling here like nathus on mired rerbok."

"Both Triads are in the Council Room, my lady," Trin said, her eyes wide in her grey face. "Not a whisper why. None whatever!"

"Both Triads in the Council Room?" Caissa recognized a meeting of premier significance. No secret had ever been extracted from that shielded chamber. Further, Red Ruler had been reputed mortally ill. Yet, if he were here in Blue City and so many Cavernii congregating, an executive decision was imminent. She shook with an apprehensive seizure as devastating as largefever. "I'll change and see what I can learn from my sire." She *had* to know what was happening from Baythan for Murell's and the coelura's sakes.

She hesitated as she unfastened the garment that Murell had touched. With reluctant hands, she stripped it off and watched Trin bundle the clothing aside. Caissa had herself well composed by the time Trin had dressed her appropriately.

The many-leveled Blue Tower was a massive ziggurat, its square base eight kilometers broad, its subterranean facilities even broader. The upper tiers with their fine, far views were reserved for ranking residents but even the serving classes had windows. The public facilities included an enormous Hall off which lay the shielded Council Room and the Rulers' private quarters and offices as well as an immense Function Room where the favored could promenade, enjoying spectacular views of forest, cliff and sea. Amenities such as dining alcoves for large or small parties, dancing and entertainment arenas were situated on levels adjacent to the Public Complex.

When Caissa reached the Function Room, it was crowded. She had never seen her languid peers so animated. She ought to have enjoyed that evening for rumor and speculation raised conversations out of the platitudinous to the provocative and amusing. But she found herself falling into reveries of her encounter with Murell. She re-examined every nuance and word, every caress and glance. She couldn't concentrate on what anyone said to her, no matter how witty or outrageous. Nor could she find her sire among the milling horde of elegant people. Curiously enough, no one inquired from her of his health or whereabouts. She didn't at first notice that omission, being required to greet visiting Cavernii and parry their urgent queries as to the Council's extraordinary invocation. She even remembered to laugh as if she ought to know and couldn't tell. Finally, she gave up searching for Baythan, to find herself looking out to the northeast. Surely that was a coincidence but she permitted herself to gaze long into the twilight distance, seeing but not seeing the lights of transports homing in on the Blue City Tower.

Then she had to admit that she might be just slightly infatuated by Murell. Although she'd experienced that sort of shallow lustfulness before, her thoughts of Murell dwelt less on the sensuality of that brief relationship and more on the concepts exchanged and her intense desire to see him just once more. While loving, they had continued to converse, silent only when their mutual need demanded satiation. But they had talked with rare candidness, in total empathy, one with the other, for that short night. How different Murell had been, mused Caissa, sighing as she forced herself back to the social exigencies of the company she now graced.

Then she saw her sire, making his way quickly towards her through the crowds. He had a compliment for her film-mist costume. The hazy dress was the nearest thing in her wardrobe to coelura. Indeed she ached within her fashionable mist for the rare and personal touch of coelura: Murell's coelura, a garment that fitted the wearer as more than skin and soul!

"The Cavernus Gustin met you?" Baythan's expression was politely attentive. Nor did his eyes betray more than a casual interest in her answer.

"I met him, my sire, and rejected him as well as his casket of badly cut bluestones!" Caissa allowed contempt to seep into her formal words.

"Too bad," said Baythan insincerely. "Look about you, my dear heir. The best and the worst are gathered. Including some you may not have previously encountered."

Caissa inclined her head. "Was your

hunt productive?" she asked, feigning indifference to the answer.

"My hunting gave me great satisfaction." The quiet note in his voice, the slight raising of his chest, the tiniest suspicion of a glint in his eyes told Caissa more than she wanted to know.

"Oh?"

"Yes, my heir. Look for a Cavernus to please you — just long enough to supply your need."

He smoothly glided past her towards an important Caverna and her escort. Caissa knew that Baythan had told her all he intended her to know.

And she desperately needed to know more. She must discover with whom he had hunted that previous day, where he had been hunting lately. She questioned his usual companions discreetly but each thought Baythan had hunted with someone else.

"He does hunt solitary sometimes, Caissa," one frequent comrade told her. "Says it's more sporting for the prey if he's got no back-up. Reckless of him, but that's Baythan!"

She left the Function Room then and returned to her own quarters. With the basest and best of motives, she used her sire's code to check on his speedster. All flights were entered in the Blue Tower's air traffic control but the log of Baythan's craft told her nothing. Distance travelled, mechanical servicing required, fuel used but all his flights were entered for the hunting preserves. Which, as Caissa knew, did not indicate his actual destinations.

She wished she could ease her terrible fear that her sire had been hunting coelura. Though how he could, she didn't understand. Murell had seemed to think that there had been no illegal visitations to the interdicted Oriolis. But then, he had been wrecked on that island for weeks. Caissa reviewed her sire's interests during that period. She checked his daily log and appointments and he had, as usual, been hunting. Unless he had to attend either the Blue or Red Ruler, Baythan had hunted some part of every day for years.

The next week was one of dreadful suspense for Caissa. Though Baythan did not permit her any private conversation, he watched her so intently that she had to affect interest in the various Cavernii to whom he introduced her and appear to be enjoying the festivities. Then it was announced that the privy negotiations of the two Rulers had been concluded. No more than that but the atmosphere turned electric, a current of jubilation rather than apprehension. Caissa's fear for the coelura mounted in direct proportion to the lack of more explicit detail.

On the eighth morning after her return to Blue City, Baythan presented himself at her quarters, dressed in the skin-fitting attire he customarily wore daytimes when not hunting.

"I am entering a contract with a Caverna," he told her casually. Then smiled as he glanced down at the resolution of the labyrinth game. "Well done, my dear Caissa. As my body-heir, you will favor me by being present at the ceremonial signing. Rather a choice, if unexpected, contract for me," he said, glancing at his reflection in the mirrors.

Caissa knew that she was expected to believe that his contract was spontaneous but she did not. Too many ploys had been cast at her sire on Demeathorn for him to acquiesce so amiably during this past week. Her anxiety for the coelura intensified.

"An heir-contract is being entered," he went on, more concerned about the small pucker across his lower back than his body-heir's opinion. "She's young and needs guidance for her heir," and Baythan favored Caissa with a doting smile. "I shall expect you to make allowances for that. She's never resided in either city. Rather a good move on my part. Good hunting in her area. Brilliant, you might say. You'll know the whole of it soon enough, Caissa. Meanwhile, deny any rumors."

"Of course, sire," she managed to say through taut lips.

"You never disappoint me, Caissa. You are as discreet as stone."

Caissa lowered her eyelids in acceptance of that barbed compliment.

"You would do well to follow my example and secure a Cavernus for yourself. There must be one man on Demeathorn you could endure for the time it takes to get an heir."

With that, he gave her a formal leave-taking and strode out.

Caissa was shattered. What her father had not said, not even the name of the Caverna nor her area, confirmed suspicions that Baythan would have no way of knowing she entertained. Somehow her sire had encountered the Oriolis Caverna and persuaded the unsophisticated and sheltered girl to enter an heir-contract. And that heir-contract must include benefits and concessions which caused the two Rulers to meet in extraordinary council. Quite likely to remove the interdiction and sanctions on Oriolis. Caissa comprehended with a sickness in her soul that was close to active nausea that one of those concessions would concern coelura. She trembled now with disgust that it was her sire's machinations that would endanger coelura.

Yet Murell had told her, several times,

that coelura were safe. Had he not also indirectly hinted that the Oriolis isolation would soon end? But, if he were part of coeluran protection and had been deliberately abandoned on that island, had he walked into another trap?

She knew the coordinates of the landing strip where she had left him. She stripped off her morning wear, dialing for her speedster to be fueled and ready as she donned flying gear. She was dressed before her call got through to the hangar manager.

"I do apologize, Lady Caissa," he said with proper deference, "but no private vehicles are allowed clearance before . . ."

"You forget who I am!" Caissa did not often use rank on those in subordinate positions but she had to find Murell.

The manager stammered a repetition of his orders and added that these were issued by the Triad Rulers. Incoming traffic was thick as splodges, he said, and he didn't know where he was going to put them.

"Your problems don't interest me. I intend to hunt today!"

She disconnected, her finger trembling

as she punched the Chief Guardian's code. After some delay, he greeted her, apologizing punctiliously, but he confirmed the restriction on out-going traffic.

"The rule applies to everyone, Lady Caissa. We've never had so many people in the City and from some mighty unexpected. . . ." His line cut off.

"Origins," she murmured, finishing the Guardian's indiscreet remark. She clenched her hands until her nails made red crescents in her palms. How could she reach Murell if she couldn't leave the City?

She didn't necessarily need her own vehicle, she realized. Any one would do. In fact, the first one she could find with sufficient fuel near an exit.

She took the fast grav channel to the hangar level. Her rank got her past a nervous guard at a side entrance. Gigantic as the City's storage space was, speedsters, cars, airbuses and even cargo vessels had had to be stacked to accommodate the numbers. The Oriolis vehicles were easily identified: their designs were so antique that she wondered how their patched and mended

hulls had remained airborne. The largest one, which must have conveyed the Caverna, had been recently sprayed and its canopy was so new that it must have been a pre-contract gift. There was no vehicle close to the exit that she would consider safe to appropriate.

Then it occurred to her that if the Oriolii were here to celebrate the contract, perhaps one of them might know Murell. Three thin bands of red, yellow and blue had been his heir-tattoo. Too simple for much rank, she imagined, but enough for identification. He might even be here. She wanted to see him. She didn't dare to see him. Yet, her sire had suggested she find a Cavernus. Surely the Oriolii had more than one.

Caissa was surprised to discover that the location of the Caverna's quarters and those of the visiting Oriolii was privileged information. Using her sire's code, she did obtain their level and direction. Surely, as she would shortly be in a contractual relationship, she would have access to the Caverna's rooms.

Triad guardroids ignored her request as

well as her voiced demand. They'd been programmed for limited service and firmly recognized that limitation. Her name had not been included in their briefing.

Frustrated but undaunted, Caissa returned to her quarters. She changed into formal attire for surely Oriolii would join those gathered in the Function Room for the evening's entertainments.

She wandered through the assemblage twice before she realized there were no unknown faces and that her sire wasn't present. To her increasing dismay, she also overheard comment on all sides that, not only had the elusive Minister Baythan agreed to an heir-contract, but the Triad Rulers were to make an announcement of planetary significance at the official signing of that document. Why hadn't she told Murell of her suspicions on that island? They had only been unsubstantiated suspicions then, the conclusions of privileged fact and coincidence. She would not really have dishonored her relationship with her sire by voicing mere speculation. Or would she?

She almost cried out with relief when

her call ring tightened on her finger, indicating a message for her. Murell? She found the nearest unit in the Function hall and didn't know whether to be annoyed or relieved that Trin timorously but urgently requested her to return to her apartment for a moment.

As Trin had never before interrupted her attendance at a function, Caissa couldn't imagine what prompted the request but any excuse to leave served Caissa well. She used the fast lane, reserved for persons of her rank or official android messengers and might have missed the encounter had there been anyone else travelling at the moment. Something about the person in the slow channel opposite her caught her attention.

"Murell!"

Though he was dressed in plain service clothes and had his head averted, she knew a shock of recognition that couldn't be denied.

He glanced back as she swept by him, confirming her intuition.

"Murell! Wait!" she cried, skillfully turning and thrusting herself across the fast

channel to catch him. "Please wait! Grab hold. There's terrible danger for the coelura. Your accident might have been arranged. Please! Wait! Something has to be done!"

He had been half across into the fast channel to evade her when he paused, caught a handhold and pulled out of the stream to permit her to reach him. His face was as stern as it had been when she had admitted knowing of coelura. Since his clothing was dull as a servant's ought to be, and not coelura, she could not measure his real feelings.

"Murell, I only heard today. My sire is Baythan and has contracted with an Oriolis Caverna — with a body-heir clause for her, since I am his. And I wish I weren't for he is somehow betraying the coelura to the Triad." Did she just imagine that he was relenting towards her? "The day I met you, he'd been hinting at achieving his mission here. It must involve coelura. He cannot realize what he is doing to those glorious creatures!" She began to weep with stress, her words tumbling through the sobs she tried to control. "I tried to leave the city to warn you but no one is permitted to leave. I went to the hangar, hoping . . . but I couldn't get a craft. Then I found where the Oriolii were quartered . . ." she had his unreserved attention now, "but they are android guarded and I wasn't coded for admittance despite the contract. I've been in the Function Room but there isn't a single Oriolis present. I did try, Murell. I did *try*! If there is any way in which I can help, let me know. The coelura must not be made to spin!"

Unexpectedly, Murell captured her in his free arm and his voice soothingly repeated her name. He tilted her chin to make her look at him and then dried her tears as they drifted together in the backswirl of grav lap. She was astonished at his ministration and the kindness in his eyes.

"Be assured, Caissa, that the coelura are protected."

"The Oriolii sanction the Caverna's contract?"

Murell smiled oddly at some point over her head. "The benefits are manifold. The Oriolii may freely resume their position in

the Triad. But I will avail myself of your offer
. . ." he paused, bringing her hand to his
lips, "of support if it is needed?"

"For anything," she cried fervently,
clinging to his hands.

"We must part. Anyone could see us.
'Till tomorrow!"

He had pushed off, into the fast down
lane before she noticed the difference about
him. His right forearm and leg were no
longer bent in ill-set lines. She was relieved
for his sake, but she would have been con-
tent to see him in any condition.

She continued on to her apartment, her
body and heart alive with the joy of having
seen Murell and delivered her warning. She
refused to consider the niggling doubt that
Baythan was a far more accomplished tacti-
cian than a Caverna who had been sheltered
from galactic-scale contingencies. It was
only as she entered her reception room that
she realized Murell had said enough to reassure her but left much unexplained, especially his presence in Blue City.

Part of that was answered when Trin,
with obsequious excitement, presented her

with a shallow rectangular box of highly polished and unusually ornamented bluewood. As soon as Caissa took it, she knew what it must contain. Glancing at Trin's expectant face, she believed that Trin did, too.

"You did well to recall me, Trin."

"The Lady Caissa will open the bluewood box?" Trin's question quavered with expectation.

Caissa would have preferred privacy to savor the thrill of coelura but to deny Trin who had served her so long would have been ungracious, and uncharacteristic behavior in herself.

As her fingers fumbled with the intricately carved fastening of the box, they triggered the lock's message.

"With this I discharge all debt."

Caissa almost dropped the gift at the implacable tone of Murell's voice. Had she not chanced to see and speak with him, that message, piercing her heart as it did despite their meeting, would have compelled her in honor never to open the box.

Now she could and did. Within the

bluewood lay coelura fabric, palely quies-
cent until she touched the folds.

"You must put it on immediately, Lady
Caissa," Trin said in an awed whisper.
"Only then will the spin live!" She stepped
back to indicate that only Caissa could
touch the length.

Caissa experienced ambivalent feelings
of reluctance and desire for an acquisition
that she had never anticipated. With shak-
ing hands, she put the box down and lifted
out the delicate length of coelura spin. She
glanced questioningly at the old dresser.

"Wrap it about your body. It will fit itself," said Trin.

Caissa obeyed and suddenly the fabric
was alive with shimmering color, smoothly
creeping across her breasts and shoulders,
snugging into her waist and down her hips
to lap about her legs.

"Be ceremonial, Lady Caissa," whispered Trin, her hands clasped tightly under
her chin, her eyes enormous with delight in
her grey face.

Regally, Caissa lifted her chin, squared
her shoulders and pulled in her diaphragm,

realizing for a fleeting miserable second that she copied that movement from her sire. Red spilled through the fabric and it ceased to cling to her legs but fell in graceful drapes to the floor. Then the color settled to echo the pattern of her heir-tattoo. Caissa, with an arrogant expression, moved across the floor in the haughty gliding pace that she had been trained to assume for the greater ceremonials. So she would walk tomorrow. And in this robe!

She could not maintain that cold imperiousness for long, not with the exultation she felt. Laughing uninhibitedly, she started to twirl in gladness, revelling in the comfort of the coelura against her bare skin. The fabric responded to her mood in pulsing reds and purples, shot with cerulean blues, breaking into spontaneous patterns as her steps fell into different dance modes. She exercised a hundred while Trin laughed and applauded until, exhausted by her excess, Caissa collapsed on her bed. Now the gown sobered and lovingly warmed her.

"You'd best sleep in it tonight, Lady Caissa, so that it knows you, or tomor-

row . . ." Trin's expression was solemn. "If the Triads should learn that you've received a coelura robe. . . . Oh, I don't know what I should do, my lady!" Trin's hands pressed against her mouth in fear.

"No one will know, Trin. And they couldn't take it from me if they did know," replied Caissa staunchly. She hugged herself and coelura lapped protectingly over her forearms. "They can never take it from me!"

"Yes, the gown would die with you, my lady, but I wouldn't want things to get that far," cried Trin.

"How long have you known about coelura, Trin?" Caissa suddenly thought to ask.

"Oh, dressers like me, we've always known about coelura. I never thought to see it in my lifetime." Trin shook her head slowly in wonder. "Tomorrow, when your sire signs that contract, you'll outshine everyone else!" That prospect seemed to offer Trin tremendous satisfaction.

Caissa could not admit to sharing a similar anticipation. Since the occasion was her sire's, her attitude was unworthy.

"Tonight you sleep in the coelura, Lady Caissa," Trin repeated. "Tomorrow no one will know it's coelura unless you let 'em."

Tomorrow, reflected Caissa, everyone will know about coelura. And someone will think to inform the High Lady Cinna. The irony that she should possess coelura before her womb-mother was doubled by the fact that a person like Lady Cinna was the greatest danger to coelura. Her robe gently compressed about Caissa's body, as if in sympathy as well as understanding.

Murell had said, Caissa reminded herself firmly, that coelura would be protected. He had emphasized that. She only hoped that he knew what he was talking about. Did he, could he, appreciate how dangerous Baythan could be so close to a long-awaited fulfillment?

The exhaustion of the day's emotional stress overcame her. Despite her anxieties, or perhaps because she was enveloped in coelura, Caissa slept.

She woke, unexpectedly refreshed, her coelura a gentle green, a shade that illuminated her lovely complexion and complemented her black hair. Trin arrived with a tray of food and exclaimed with approval at her mistress's subtly enhanced beauty.

"You'd better eat well, my lady. It's going to be a long day and with everything, you can't risk coming over faint from lack of food." Nourishment was an answer-all for Trin. "Coelura would give you away for certain if you aren't feeling well."

The food did quiet the roiling in her stomach and Caissa ate more than she intended. She did not like surrendering the gown even for bathing and it clung lovingly to her hand until she, following Murell's example, told it to behave. She kept its dulled green length in sight as she submitted to Trin's ministrations. She sighed with relief when she could settle the coelura back about her shoulders.

"Now set it in your colors, Lady Caissa."

She did and Trin could find no fault in shade, shape or drape.

"You'll never want for the perfect gown again, my lady," said Trin. "It's only just too bad as you aren't the important contractee today in that robe. You'd have all eyes. No one would outshine you."

"Outshining has never been my ambition, Trin, as well you know."

"I know," and Trin's deep sigh bordered insolent regret, "but not for my want of trying. You shine now! I'll watch it all." She activated the wall screen and tuned it to the Great Hall, now a lucent white as befitted the occasion.

Trin's excitement was nothing to the aura exuded by the invited and chosen as they moved towards the Great Hall in the slow grav stream, decorously, so as not to disarrange their finery. The entry ways from all grav channels were lined with mirrors to permit last minute adjustments before entering. Caissa's robe remained in immaculate folds about her as she stepped onto the platform. She moved politely forward in the press and pretended to touch up her hair as she glanced at the throng pausing or passing her. Everyone was, as usual, far too occupied in their own appearance to notice anything unusual about hers. She waited in the anteroom as long as she could,

hoping to locate Murell. He might have chosen to dress in lower caste neutrals to deliver her coelura yesterday but he did have an heir-tattoo. Surely he possessed rank enough to enter the Great Hall for the contracting of his Caverna.

The Great Hall was filling: the hour for the ceremony and the Triads' announcement near. Already the upper tiers were occupied by the ranking Cavernii and their body-heirs. Ambassadors and ministers from other planetary systems occupied booths and tanks or the balcony for oxygen breathers. Caissa thought wryly that her sire was certainly going to achieve maximum dissemination of his new contract as well as his mission's success.

Although she had no part in the ceremony, she was his body-heir and would stand the usual three steps behind him, to his right. She moved across the immense Hall to take her position on the lowest of the four steps leading up to the two ceremonial chairs, red and blue, set for the Triad Rulers. There was, she noticed, sufficient room for a third chair on that dais.

With slow dignity, she viewed the assembled and, though she had often been a witness to prestigious contracts, she had never seen the Hall so crowded. Black guardroids kept open an aisle down which her sire would lead his new contract partner.

The sonic call-to-order peeled melodiously, through the Hall to the subtly carved domed ceiling. Before the last echo had died, two notes summoned the Rulers of the Blue and Red Triad cities. There should be three, thought Caissa rebelliously. For surely the Yellow City would be reinstated and Demeathorn united in its original Triadic form.

She had always known that the two Rulers were old but suddenly she realized how old they must be for unmistakably both wore coelura robes. She knew Blue Ruler to be in his fifteenth decade and Red Ruler was older. Blue Ruler's gown was vibrant, sparkling; Red Ruler's blurred. She remembered the gossip that Red Ruler had not completely recovered from his recent illness. His robe, now that she had some grasp of the properties of coelura, gave the strength to that report. Red Ruler's body-heir now took his place and his garment, rich though it was, was a poor imitation of what his sire wore. He would need a coelura robe to maintain the dignity and authority of his office. How much compromise had been extracted from the obdurate Oriolii who had withstood sanctions for so long? Had the need for a new Ruler's robe been an advantage? And for whom?

Her robe began to shimmer and she hastily depressed her thoughts. The sonics trilled again, announcing the entrance of her sire and the Oriolis Caverna.

Simultaneously Caissa observed two things: her sire was wearing coelura that rippled in muddy colors, vibrating disappointment or suppressed anger. Secondly, his partner, as beautiful and graceful as a Caverna ought to be, was also in distress but she was maintaining the striped pattern of blue, red and yellow. Nothing in Baythan's noble bearing, his firm stride courteously shortened to match the Caverna's, would indicate that all was not as it should be. Then his clothing settled into a firmer pat-

tern of his colors but Caissa knew that Baythan, Minister Plenipotential, was under
stress. Sufficient for his heir to realize that
Baythan was not having everything his own
way. Sufficient, Caissa hoped, not to notice
his heir's costume was unusual.

Casual contracts or those between lower
ranks were duly registered on the Memorax,
but for persons of ministerial or cavernii
status, documents were handscribed on a
carefully treated paper which would instantly change color if tampered with after
the final signing.

Baythan's chief aide presented the large
and beautifully detailed contract to the Blue
Triadic Ruler who made a show of reading
before passing it to Red Ruler. Red Ruler's
body-heir stepped forward and spoke to his
sire. Red Ruler looked more closely at the
document and rose to his feet, assisted by
his heir.

"There is no mark," the old man said in a
clear but forceless voice, "or mention that
this Contract has been approved by the Oriolis Cavernus."

Baythan's robe streaked with grey,

flushed to the red of embarrassment though Baythan obviously controlled his private anger more quickly than he could his garment. The Caverna swayed, the blues and reds of her gown attacked by the yellow stripes, travelling from heart to hem.

"Gracious Rulers," Baythan began, "the Cavernus Murell . . ."

"The Cavernus Murell is present!"

It was Caissa's turn to sway, but joy and surprise merely deepened the pattern of her coelura to a pulsing brilliance noticeable to all close to her. Baythan had whirled at Murell's carrying voice, instinctively supporting the Caverna with his left arm. Whether the girl had had any part in Murell's crash, Caissa would never know and later doubted. The Caverna collected herself quickly as she turned towards the aisle.

"I thought you dead, Murell!" Her voice rang with a relief and amazement which was, Caissa credited her by her robe, probably genuine. She would have rushed to the figure striding in the magnificence of coelura stripes, but Baythan's grasp recalled her to the proprieties.

"My profound apologies for this belated appearance, gracious Rulers," and Murell made an obeisance, just proper for a Cavernus before a Ruler, yet something about his person—his robes—lent him an air and authority equal to that of the Triadic Rulers. "My vehicle, doubtless due to worn parts, crashed seven weeks ago and was so damaged that no signal indicated my position. When my injuries were sufficiently healed, I returned to my Cavern. I have but just learned of your gracious consent to reinstate the Oriolii." Then he stepped beside the Caverna who stared fixedly at him.

Red Ruler smartly extended the contract to Murell who bowed before accepting it.

"That document is valid only if the Caverna is both Oriolis heir and body-heir," said Red Ruler firmly, sternly glancing at Blue Ruler who affected polite dismay.

Holding the paper by top and bottom, Murell appeared to study the paragraphs, his expression politely intent, but Caissa was positive that he had known its contents beforehand and had carefully timed his unexpected arrival.

"A minor addition will validate it since I am Cavernus and Oriolis body-heir." Murell turned now and, for the first time, acknowledged the presence of Baythan with a very correct bow. "I certainly have no wish to protest such a distinguished connection or deprive the Caverna of the wisdom and advice of your Excellency as her contractual partner, one so keenly interested in Oriolii welfare.

"However," and Murell turned back to the two Rulers, "as Cavernus and body-heir, rank and duty compel me to be First Comptroller in all matters pertaining to coelura spin." There was a stir of suppressed excitement and shock in the audience. Murell bowed. "You will find my administration impartial since I have no prejudice for those along the Base of the Triangle. It profits neither your two Cities nor Oriolii to continue an isolation for a cause that no longer exists. The species 'coelura' are secure."

Red and Blue Rulers leaned together across the gap between their chairs. Blue Ruler's shoulders were hunched with the urgency of the arguments he made to Red

Ruler. Caissa spared a glance at her sire and saw that his colors were remarkably settled, his face composed. She admired his containment at what must be a severe check to his ambitions for there was little doubt in Caissa's mind that Baythan intended, through the Caverna, to control coelura spins. He turned his head slightly, his lips moving in a phrase audible only to the Caverna. The girl blinked once, the only indication of surprise before her lips formed the negative. Baythan relaxed and the slight tilt of satisfaction in the set of his shoulders made Caissa wonder what her sire's cunning mind had devised at this juncture.

The two Rulers had ended their conference and Red Ruler asked that the writer be summoned. Then he gestured to the assembled, giving permission for them to speak quietly among themselves.

Caissa could not quit her position and there was no one near enough with whom she could have conversed had she been of that mind. Except Murell. And she couldn't acknowledge him yet. Murell now came down the step to her sire. Baythan, with a

gracious smile, extended his hand. As if released from a paralysis, the Caverna clutched at Murell's right arm with both hands, her face turned up to his, her lips moving rapidly, explaining many things as fast as she could. Murell covered her hands with his, his manner reassuring. Baythan exchanged a few more words with Murell who regarded the Minister for a long moment. Caissa saw Murell ask one single quiet question and then her sire gestured towards her.

Caissa exerted every ounce of self-control to keep her gown from responding to the leap of emotion that surged through her. Murell inclined his head in her direction and then bowed formally to Baythan.

At this point, the writer, with assistants carrying his tall table and casket of writing implements, appeared from the Triadic offices. Baythan beckoned Caissa, his expression politely but earnestly entreating. She knew with a joy that did cause her robe to shimmer what her sire wanted of her. She almost burst out laughing at the irony. Baythan would not find her so compliant if he tried to override Murell in the matter of coelura.

"Caissa, as my body-heir, I have the right to request you to consider your first contract to further our mutual interests."

Caissa acknowledged that right.

"Would you consent to a contract with Cavernus Murell? I can assure you that the privileges of such a contract far outweigh any other that I have recommended to you."

Caissa made the filial obeisance before she looked at Murell. She was very nearly undone by the twinkle of his eyes.

"What form of contract, my sire?"

"With so much at issue, Baythan," said Murell, "I must insist on a body contract of five standard years to ensure the health of that heir."

Baythan was visibly startled. Caissa knew that he must be rapidly assessing the value of this double commitment to the Oriolii, whether it would improve or hamper his own designs and whether he dared insist that Caissa approve such a long heir-contract.

"Sire Baythan," said Caissa, drawling.

She pretended to study Murell's face and figure with a calculating eye. "I should be an undutiful heir not to do everything in my power to support you at this moment." But her eyes sought Murell's as she spoke.

The fingers of her sire's right hand twitched briefly in recognition of her unexpected capitulation. Baythan gave Caissa a sudden searching look of suspicion before he, too, smiled with every evidence of pride in her filial submission. He took a step forward to get the attention of the two Rulers, approaching to make his request. Caissa, who dared not look at Murell when her heart was singing as loudly as coelura, watched the faces of the Rulers. She thought that Red Ruler smiled as he listened to Baythan.

"You wear coelura," whispered the Caverna to Caissa in the accomplished voiceless way of their rank.

"A life-debt, my lady," Caissa replied and smiled at the girl who would now be in a double relationship to her.

The Caverna's eyebrows puckered slightly in perplexity.

"When I whistled coelura to spin two lengths, I thought one was to fulfill a contract debt."

Both girls heard Murell's chuckle.

"No, a life-debt, Anvral," said Murell.

"*You* rescued Murell." Anvral shot a look of gratitude to Caissa and then one of anger to the Cavernus. "Why didn't you let me know?"

"After my 'accident,' discretion seemed the wiser course. You were proceeding very well, Anvral, without my assistance." Murell's eyes gleamed with friendly malice.

Then Baythan raised his hands for silence. He announced the double contract. As the Great Hall buzzed with agitation, Murell was beckoned forward. The two Rulers, Murell and Baythan watched the writer amend the document.

"How did you meet Baythan?" Caissa had a few questions of her own.

"*He* rescued *me*," said Anvral, her eyes crinkling with laughter though she kept her face composed, "from an amphibian when I was searching for Murell. Are rescue missions to interdicted areas a genetic trait in your line?"

"My sire is known to be fortunate," Caissa replied with discreet sincerity. This girl was not as unsophisticated as Baythan had been led to believe.

"Caverna Anvral," said Blue Ruler, "body-heir Lady Caissa, your signatures are required."

"I would like to scan the document first," said Caissa as she approached the writing table.

"A wise lady," said Red Ruler with a hint of a smile tugging at his sad lips.

Caissa knew enough about such contracts to flick through the first paragraphs about obligation, responsibility, damages and sanctions applicable if the obligations were not fulfilled. The paragraph concerning her sire and Anvral gave two years of body-heir provision. In small but quite legible script, the writer had added the conditions stipulated by Murell.

The third paragraph she read slowly for it outlined the end of the interdiction of the Oriolii and stated that coelura fabric would

again be available for export and at a price
per spin that made Caissa's eyes widen.
Murell's name had been substituted for
Anvral's as Comptroller. Official garments
would be supplied to ranking Cavernii (so
that had been Baythan's reason for her to
contract), Triadic Rulers and their body-
heirs at need and at no expense. Yellow
Triad City was to be restored, an enormous
credit balance advanced to replenish and
refurbish Oriolii Caverns and surface facilities. Yellow Triad Ruler was to be nominated
by the Oriolis Cavernii, that candidate to be
accepted by Red and Blue Rulers. The writer
had added only one line to this clause: the
supply of coelura fabric would not exceed
one spin per adult coelura in any Demeathorn year.

Caissa raised her eyes in appeal to Murell for she could not see how such a restriction could be enforced. Surely there would
be attempts to capture the beautiful and
friendly creatures and remove them from
Demeathorn, after which they could be
forced to spin themselves to death. Murell
returned her gaze serenely. In soft caress,

her gown hugged closer to her body and she understood that to be reassurance.

She signed above her scribed name, handing the pen to Anvral. Murell affixed his signature beside hers as Baythan put his next to Anvral's. Both Rulers signed and Red Ruler held the document high.

"We pronounce this double contract valid and inviolable," he said, his voice issuing firmly, "honorably to be discharged by Cavernus Murell and Lady Caissa, and by Caverna Anvral and His Excellency, Baythan." He motioned to the newly contracted to join hands. "Let us now celebrate the glad occasion of a reunited continent and an equilateral triangle."

Cheering followed as the two Rulers retired to their offices. The massive stairway to the Function Room on the upper level began to open, stirring the audience to rearrange themselves and ascend.

Caissa turned anxiously to Murell.

"No fears, Caissa. Coelura are safe." Murell smiled warmly down at her and pressed her hands together in his. "Both Anvral and I have been as carefully trained for this transaction as the coelura. Over the past one hundred and twenty years, the coelura have been conditioned to respond only to a certain combination of notes known to a trusted minority. With myself as Comptroller and Anvral committed to Baythan . . ." Murell glanced over Caissa's shoulder towards Anvral and her sire when his grasp tightened on her fingers. The quality of his smile altered. "So this is the other contract spin," he said and abruptly swung Caissa towards the milling guests.

Caissa could not suppress her gasp of amazement at the sight of the High Lady Cinna, gliding ruthlessly towards them. Even in a stunning gathering of the ultra-fashionable, Lady Cinna was outstandingly garbed, her costume composed of the highly prized and costly imbia shells of a nascent gold. Her hair, dyed a subtly darker shade, had been dressed in long thin plaits, studded with tinier shells. The effect was dazzling until she neared the newly contracted couples.

"My sincerest congratulations, Minister Baythan," she said in her most brittle and indolent voice, more like the sly nathus than ever. "Quite a coup, in fact. I presume you have not forgotten. . . ."

Caissa caught her breath, swallowing down a taste of bile at the thought of the High Lady Cinna swathed in coelura.

"How could one forget you, Lady Cinna!" exclaimed Baythan, his voice as smoothly composed as the colors of his robe. Somehow a bluewood box appeared in his hand. He spared a sideways look at Caissa and she must have imagined that her sire winked. "A small token by which to remember sire and heir."

"May it become you," Caissa added, stepping with Murell to Baythan's right.

In a daze, Lady Cinna's hands closed about the box. Her expression turned from smug anticipation to irate dismay as she appraised the vibrant gowns which dulled her magnificence to insipid beige.

Her eyes narrowed with fury, and frustration pulled lines in her face which discipline and surgery had long disguised. The imbia shells shook with her suppressed rage.

"Honor being satisfied, my heir, let us celebrate," said Baythan, bowing formally to the motionless High Lady and escorting Anvral towards the festivities.

Murell led Caissa away, the drape of their gowns enmeshing as his fingers pressed hers with the promise of renewing their first encounter.

"Lady Cinna really deserves coelura," Murell remarked with droll humor in his deep voice. "It *will* become her, you know!"

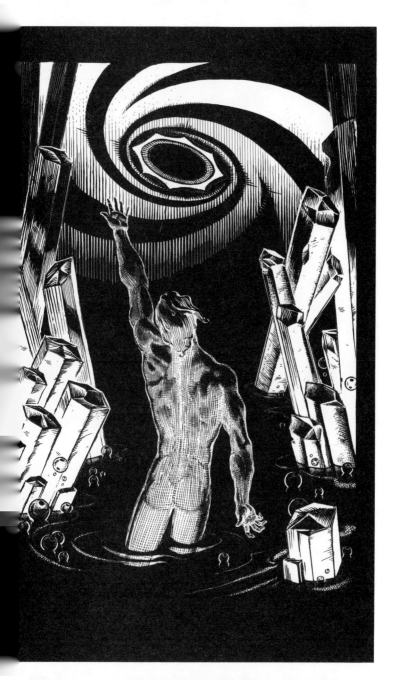

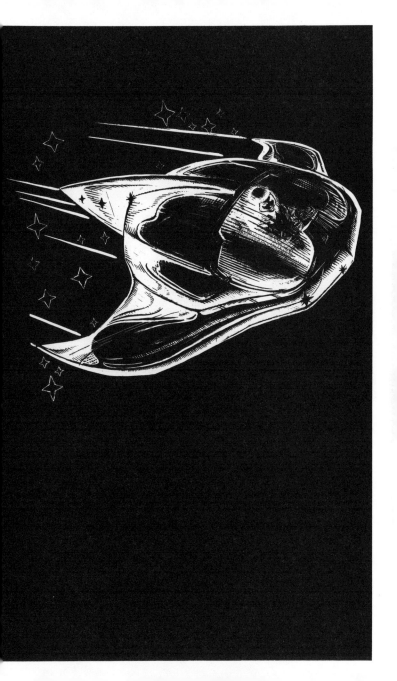